# READ WITH ME
# STORIES

ADAPTED BY LUCY KINCAID

ILLUSTRATED BY ERIC KINCAID • GILLIAN EMBLETON

ERIC ROWE • BELINDA LYON

BRIMAX BOOKS • NEWMARKET • ENGLAND

# CONTENTS

# Snow White
## and the Seven Dwarfs

Once there was a wicked Queen who
had a magic mirror. Every day she
would say,
"Mirror, mirror on the wall,
Who is the fairest of them all?"
Every day the mirror would reply,
"You, oh Queen,
Are the fairest in all the land."

One day, the Queen asked,
"Mirror, mirror on the wall,
Who is the fairest of them all?"
And the mirror replied,
"You, oh Queen, are very fair,
But Snow White is the fairest in
all the land."
Instead of her
own face looking
from the mirror
the Queen saw the
face of her step-
daughter. She was
VERY angry.

She sent for her huntsman. "Take
Snow White into the forest and
kill her," she said.

The huntsman loved Snow White. "I
cannot kill you," he said. "But
I cannot take you home either. You
must stay here, in the forest."

The huntsman returned to the palace
alone. He told the Queen he had
killed Snow White.

Snow White wandered through the dark forest. She did not know where to go, or what to do. Presently she came to a little house. "Perhaps the people who live here will help me," she said. She knocked at the door. There was no reply, so she peeped inside.

What an untidy house it was. Every
thing in it was smaller than usual.
And there seemed to be seven of
EVERYTHING. Seven chairs. Seven
beds. Seven spoons. Seven plates.
Seven mugs. Seven of EVERYTHING
. . . except tables. There was just
one table.

"Perhaps children who have lost
their mother live here," said
Snow White. "I will tidy the
house for them."

She swept, and dusted and cleaned
and polished. She had plenty of
helpers.

There was a diamond mine on the
far side of the forest. It was
worked by seven dwarfs. The very
same dwarfs who lived in the house
Snow White had found. They were
on their way home. What would
happen to Snow White now?

"Who . . . who are you?" asked Snow White. "This is our house," said the seven dwarfs all together. "We work in the diamond mine on the far side of the forest. Do not be afraid, we will not hurt you. Just tell us what are YOU doing in OUR house?"

Snow White told the dwarfs what had happened.

"You can stay here with us. We will look after you." said the dwarfs.

"And I will look after you," said Snow White. "I will cook and sew and clean for you."

And she did. And they were all very happy.

But the dwarfs were afraid the wicked Queen would come looking for Snow White one day. "Do not answer the door to anyone," they said, whenever they went to the mine.

They were right to be worried.

"Mirror, mirror on the wall,
Who is the fairest of them all?"
asked the Queen.
"You, oh Queen, are very fair,
But Snow White, who lives in the
forest with the little men, is
the fairest in all the land."
The Queen was VERY ANGRY
INDEED. "I will kill Snow White
myself!" she said.

The Queen disguised herself as a pedlar. She filled a basket with apples then went into the forest. She waited until the dwarfs had gone to the mine, then she knocked at the door of the little house. "I have nothing to fear from a pedlar," said Snow White. And though the dwarfs had warned her not to open the door, she did.

"Good day child," said the Queen.
"Would you like one of my apples?"
"Yes please . . ." said Snow White.
The Queen gave
Snow White the
reddest apple in
the basket. It
was a special
apple. A VERY
special apple.
The Queen had
put a spell on
it.

"Take a bite . . ." said the Queen.
Snow White took just one bite from
the apple and fell to the floor.
"Ha! Ha!" laughed the Queen, and
she threw off her disguise.
"Snow White is dead. Now I am
the fairest in all the land!"

When the dwarfs came home they found Snow White lying on the floor. They found the apple, with one bite taken from it, lying beside her. "The wicked Queen has been here," they said sadly. "Snow White is dead!"

The dwarfs built a special bed for Snow White in the forest. The birds and the animals kept watch around her.

One day a prince came riding by and saw her lying there.
"Please let me take her home," he said.

As the Prince lifted Snow White onto his horse she opened her eyes. The piece of magic apple had fallen from her throat. The spell cast by the wicked Queen was broken. "Snow White is alive!" shouted the dwarfs. "Hoorah! Hoorah!"

Once more, the Queen asked the magic mirror who was the fairest of them all.

The mirror replied,

"You, oh Queen, are very fair,
But Snow White, the Prince's bride,
is the fairest in all the land."

The Queen was so angry, she flew into a rage and died herself. And so Snow White was safe at last.

All these appear in the pages of
the story. Can you find them?

Queen

mirror

Snow White

huntsman

wood

dwarfs

apple

Prince

Use the pictures to tell the story
in your own words, and then draw
your own pictures.

# The Ugly Duckling

Mother Duck had five broken egg shells, and five new ducklings. She had one egg which did not have a crack in it.

"I wonder when that egg will hatch," said Mother Duck.

Everyone who lived in the farmyard
came to look at the egg.
"That is too big to be a duck's
egg," said a chicken.
"That will hatch into a turkey,
you mark my words," said a goose.
"How will I know if it is a
turkey?" asked Mother Duck.
"It will not swim," said the
goose.

At last the egg hatched. The bird which stepped from the broken shell did not look like his brothers and sisters at all. But he was not a turkey for he went straight to the pond and began to swim.

"What an ugly
little duckling
you are," laughed
the chickens.

"What an ugly
little duckling
you are," laughed
the geese.
"What an ugly
little duckling
you are," laughed
the other ducks.

The little duckling was so unhappy.
He had no friends. EVERYONE laughe
at him, even his mother.
He decided to run away. "Nobody
will miss me," he said. And
nobody did.

He made his home on the marshes.
One day he saw some wild ducks
swimming in a pool. "Will you be
my friends?" he asked.
"What an ugly little duckling you
are," laughed the wild ducks. "We
do not want you in our pool."
They chased him away.

One day the little duckling saw
some swans flying across the sky.
"I wish I were a swan," he said.
"Swans are beautiful. Nobody laughs
at them." He felt sadder than
ever as he watched them fly away.

Winter came. The days were cold. The nights were even colder. Food was very hard to find.

Now the little duckling was not only lonely, he was cold and hungry too.

One cold night the lake froze.
When morning came the duckling's
feet were stuck firmly in the ice.
He could not move.
"Now I will die," he said.
A farmer was taking his dog for a
walk. He saw the duckling stuck
in the ice.
"We must get you out of there,"
he said.
The farmer broke the ice with a
stick. The little duckling was
free again.

"Go and find your
friends," said the
farmer.
"I wish I had a
friend to find,"
said the little
duckling sadly.

The winter was very long but it did not last for ever. Spring came. The days grew warmer. There was plenty to eat. The wild ducks and the wild geese came back to the lake. They had all been away for the winter.

They dabbled and they splashed
about in the water and all
tried to talk at once.
They had so many things to tell
one another. But nobody spoke to
the little duckling.
"I wish they would talk to me,"
he said.

The little duckling
watched the wild
ducks stretch their
wings. He
stretched his own wings.
He flapped them.
And then he flew,
for the very first
time. Up, up and
up, he went, up
into the clear blue
sky.

He should have been happy, but he did not feel happy. He looked down at the ground far below him. He could see the swans swimming in a pond in a beautiful garden. He would ask them to help him.

He flew down to the pond and settled on the water. He called to the swans. "Please come and kill me. I am so ugly, and I am so lonely I do not want to live."

"Ugly? You?" said the swans looking surprised. "Have you looked at yourself in the pond?"

The little duckling looked down into the water. Looking back at him was a swan.

"Is . . . is that me?" he asked.
"Of course it is," said the swans.
"But I am beautiful," he said.
"Of course you are," said the swans.
"You are a swan. All swans are beautiful."

Three children came running to the
pond.
"Look!" they cried. "A new swan.
Please stay in our pond. We will
come and see you every day."
The little duckling had changed into
a beautiful swan during the long
cold winter. He would never be
lonely again.

All these appear in the pages of
the story. Can you find them?

Mother Duck

chicken

goose

duckling

wild duck

swan

farmer

dog

Use the pictures to tell the story
in your own words, and then draw
your own pictures.

# Sleeping Beauty

A Princess had been born at the palace.

"We must make sure she has all a Princess should have," said the King. "We must invite the fairies to her christening."

"How many fairies live in our Kingdom?" asked the Queen. "Seven," said the King. "We must invite them all." So the King sent invitations to each one. The King had seven golden caskets made as gifts for the seven fairies.

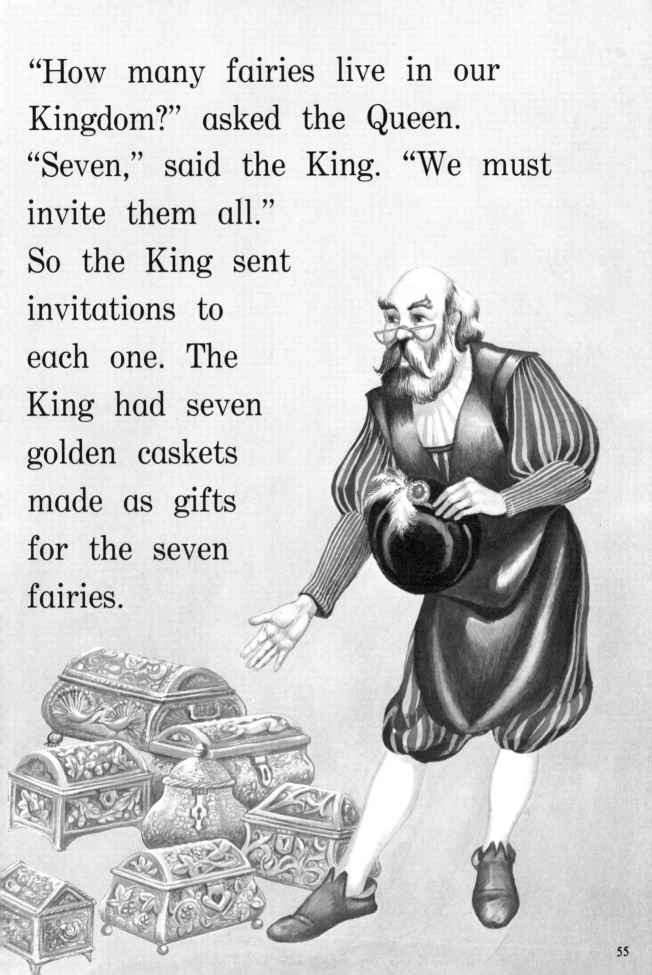

The day of the christening came. All the guests were sitting in the great palace hall. Suddenly the door flew open. Standing in the doorway was a very angry fairy.

"That is the fairy who lives at the bottom of the well," whispered the King. "I thought she had moved away. We did not send her an invitation."

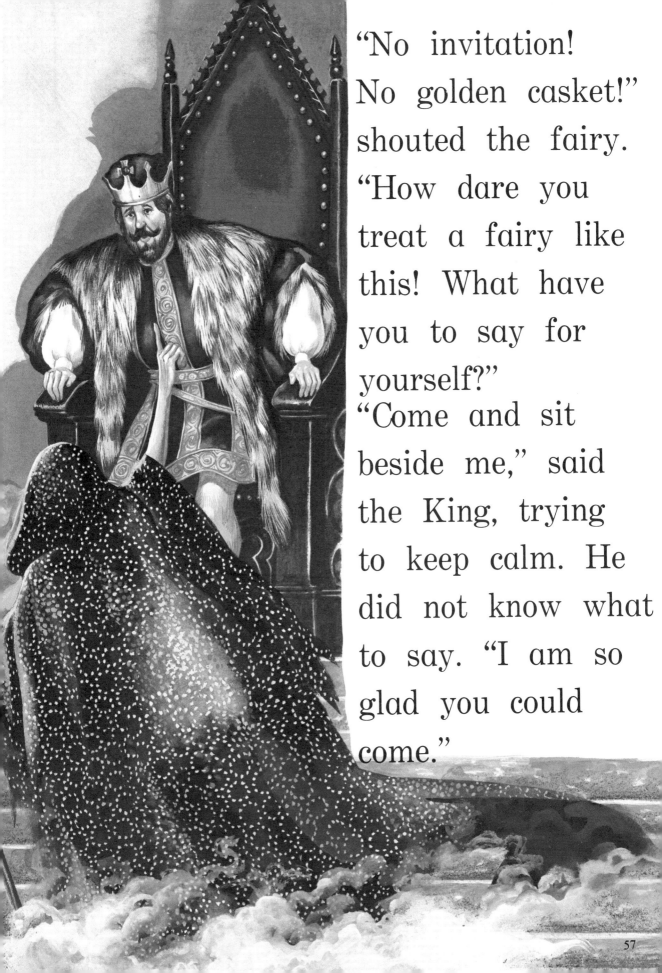

"No invitation! No golden casket!" shouted the fairy. "How dare you treat a fairy like this! What have you to say for yourself?"

"Come and sit beside me," said the King, trying to keep calm. He did not know what to say. "I am so glad you could come."

When the party was over, the fairies stood round the cradle. They had gifts for the baby Princess.

It came to the seventh fairy's turn to give the Princess a gift.

"Where is the seventh fairy?" asked the King.

"Where is the seventh fairy?" asked the Queen.

Nobody knew where she was.

"We cannot wait
for her," said the
fairy who had been
forgotten. "I want
to give my gift to
the Princess."
Everyone held his
breath. Was she
still angry?
"My gift shall be
this," said the
fairy with a sly
smile. "The
Princess shall
prick her finger
on a spindle and
DIE!"

The King and Queen wept. knew what to do. It was the seventh fairy came back. "Do not weep," she said. "I too have a gift for the Princess. She will prick her finger it is true, but she will not die. She will sleep for one hundred years instead." Everyone went home. The Queen dried her tears. The Princess slept in her cradle.

The King ordered
that all the
spindles in the
kingdom be destroyed.
"If there are no
spindles, the
Princess cannot
prick her finger
on one," he said.

Sixteen years passed. One day the Princess went for a walk. She came to a tumbledown cottage. She pushed open the door and peeped inside. There was an old woman sitting by the window. She had a spindle in her hand. She was spinning thread. "Come along in," called the old woman.

"What are you doing?" asked the Princess.

"I am spinning," said the old woman.

The Princess watched the spindle twirl.

"Would you like to twirl the spindle?" asked the old woman.

"Yes please," said the Princess. She sat by the window and took the spindle from the old woman. "Just a little faster," said the old woman. "Like this?" said the Princess. "Faster . . . faster . . ." said the old woman.

"Oh!" cried the Princess. "I have
pricked my finger." She fell to
the floor in a deep sleep. She
slept so soundly nobody could wake
her.

The seventh fairy heard what had happened to the poor Princess who was taken back to the palace and laid on her bed. The seventh fairy cast a spell that made everyone else in the palace sleep as soundly as the Princess.

"Now the Princess will not be alone when she wakes," said the fairy.

A thick, thorny hedge grew up round
the palace and hid it. The years
passed by. Strange stories were
told about what lay behind the hedge.
Many people tried to cut a way
through it, but nobody could.

One hundred years after the Princess had fallen asleep along came a Prince. The hedge seemed to melt at the touch of his sword. He could not believe what he saw. All over the palace there were people who had fallen asleep in the middle of what they had been doing.

There were cooks in the middle of cooking, maids in the middle of sweeping and pageboys in the middle of fighting. There were footmen in the middle of carrying messages, lords in the middle of talking and ladies in the middle of dressing. The Prince had to laugh.

When the Prince saw the sleeping
Princess he kissed her. She opened
her eyes and smiled at him. As
she woke the palace clocks started
ticking.

Then everyone else in the palace woke too and carried on with what they had been doing one hundred years before. They all lived happily ever after.

All these appear in the pages of the story. Can you find them?

King

Queen

Princess

cradle

fairy

cottage

spindle

hedge

Use the pictures to tell the story
in your own words, and then draw
your own pictures.

# The Elves and the Shoemaker

Once there was a shoemaker. He sat at his bench making shoes all day long. He worked very hard but nobody would pay him a fair price for the shoes he made. He and his wife were very poor.

One day, the
shoemaker showed
his wife a piece
of leather.
"This is the last
piece of leather
I have," he said.
"When it is gone
I will be unable
to make any more
shoes. We will
get very hungry.
We may even starve."
"No wonder you look so sad," said
his wife. She was sad herself.

The shoemaker cut out the pieces
for the last pair of shoes. He
put them on the bench.
"It is late," he said. "Let us
go to bed. I will sew the pieces
together in the morning."

"Wife! Wife!" he called loudly next morning. "Come quickly!"
"What is it?" cried his wife. She ran into the workshop. There on the bench was a beautiful pair of finished shoes.
"Did you get up in the night and make them?" she asked.
The shoemaker shook his head.
"Then how did they get there?" she asked.
"I do not know," said the shoemaker.

"Whoever made the shoes meant us to have them," said the shoemaker. "They would not have left them behind otherwise."

He took the shoes to market. He sold them for a very good price. He and his wife would not starve that day, or the next.

When the shoemaker had bought food, he had enough money left to buy leather for TWO more pairs of shoes.

He cut the pieces for the new shoes and laid them on the bench. "I will sew them tomorrow," he said.

"Wife! Wife! Come quickly!" called the shoemaker next morning. "It has happened again!"

"I don't believe it!" said the shoemaker's wife. There, on the bench, were two pairs of finished shoes.

"Look how well they are made," said the shoemaker. "There isn't a stitch out of place."

"Fine shoes for sale!" he cried when he got to the market place. "Fine shoes for sale!" He sold both pairs in the first five minutes he was there. He was paid a very good price for them too. That day he bought enough leather to make four more pairs of shoes.

And so it went on. Every night the shoemaker left pieces of leather on the bench. Every morning they had been sewn into shoes. Every day he bought more leather. One day, the shoemaker's wife said, "I do wish we knew who is making the shoes for us. We owe everything to them. I would like to say thank you." "I know how we can find out," said the shoemaker.

That night he put the pieces of leather on the bench as before. He put out the light, as before. But instead of going to bed, as before, the shoemaker and his wife hid in the darkest corner of the room and waited. At midnight two little elves stepped in through the open window.

They sat cross-legged on the bench
and began to sew. They did not
waste a minute. When they had put
the last stitch into the last shoe
they slipped away as quietly as
they had come.

The shoemaker and his wife hurried to the window.

"We must find a way of thanking them," said the shoemaker.

"The poor little things," said his wife. "Did you notice how ragged their clothes were? And did you notice they had no shoes?"

"I will make them shoes," said the shoemaker.

"And I will make them each a set of clothes," said his wife.

The shoemaker took the finest, softest piece of leather he had, and made two pairs of tiny shoes. He had never made anything so small before.

The shoemaker's wife took the finest cloth she could find and made two sets of tiny clothes. She knitted two pairs of tiny stockings. She made two tiny hats. She had never made anything quite so small before.

By Christmas Eve everything was ready. That night the shoemaker put all the shoe leather underneath the bench. On top of the bench he put the two pairs of tiny shoes. His wife laid the two sets of tiny clothes beside them. Then they hid and waited for the elves to come.

When the elves saw what was on the bench they cried out in delight. "These must be for us!" they said. They took off their rags and dressed themselves in their new clothes. They put on their new shoes. They put on their new hats. And all the time they smiled and smiled.

The two happy little elves danced
a merry jig all along the bench.
"Now we are no longer poor,
Cobbling we will do no more,"
they sang.
Then they skipped out through the
window and were gone.

The shoemaker and his wife never saw the elves again. But their luck had changed. The shoes the shoemaker made, sold as well as the shoes the elves had made. They were never poor again and lived happily ever after.

All these appear in the pages of
the story. Can you find them?

shoemaker

shoemaker's wife

shoes                    bench

leather                    elves

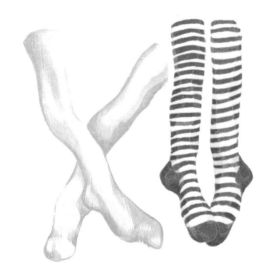

hats

stockings

Use the pictures to tell the story
in your own words, and then draw
your own pictures.

# Little Red Riding Hood

Little Red Riding Hood's mother was packing a basket with eggs and butter and homemade bread. "Who is that for?" asked Little Red Riding Hood.

"For Grandma," said Mother. "She has not been feeling well." Grandma lived alone in a cottage in the middle of the wood.

"I will take it to her," said Little Red Riding Hood. She put on her red cape with the red hood and picked up the basket.

"Make sure you go straight to the cottage," said Mother as she waved goodbye. "And do not talk to any strangers."

Little Red Riding Hood meant to go straight to the cottage but there were so many wild flowers growing in the wood, she decided to stop and pick some for Grandma. Grandma liked flowers. They would cheer her up.

"Good morning," said a voice at her elbow. It was a wolf. "Where are you taking these goodies?" he asked, peeping inside the basket.

"I am taking them to my Grandma," said Little Red Riding Hood, quite forgetting what her mother had said about talking to strangers.

"Lucky Grandma," said the wolf. "Where does she live?"

"In the cottage in the middle of the wood," said Little Red Riding Hood.

"Be sure to pick her a nice BIG bunch of flowers," said the wolf, and hurried away.

The wolf went
straight to
Grandma's cottage.
He knocked at the
door.
"Who is there?"
called Grandma.
"It is I, Little
Red Riding Hood,"
replied the wolf
in a 'little girl'
voice.
"Then lift up the
latch and come in,"
called Grandma.

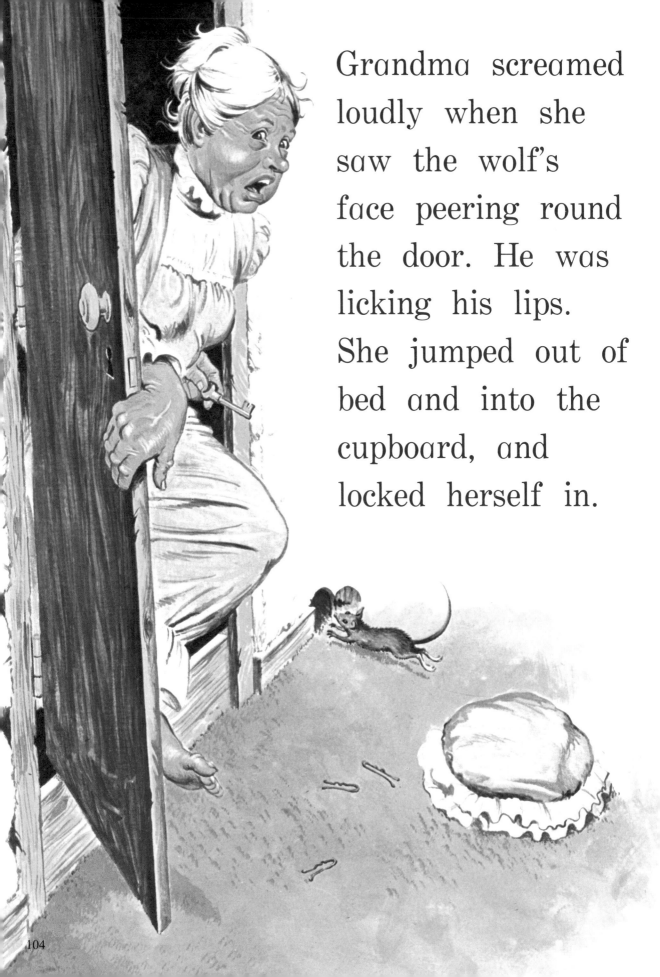

Grandma screamed
loudly when she
saw the wolf's
face peering round
the door. He was
licking his lips.
She jumped out of
bed and into the
cupboard, and
locked herself in.

The wolf picked up her frilly bed-
cap, which had fallen to the floor,
and put it on his own head. He
pushed his ears inside the cap
then climbed into Grandma's bed.
He pulled the covers up round his
neck, then sat and waited for
Little Red Riding Hood to come.

Presently, there was a knock at the door.

"Who is there?" he called, in a voice that sounded like Grandma's.

"It is I, Little Red Riding Hood," replied Little Red Riding Hood.

"Then lift up the latch and come in," called the sly, old wolf.

Little Red Riding
Hood lifted the
latch and went in.
"Are you feeling
better, Grandma?"
she asked.

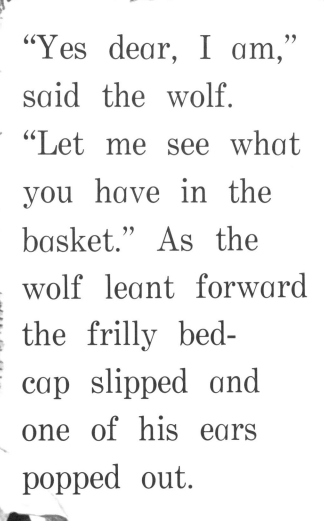

"Yes dear, I am,"
said the wolf.
"Let me see what
you have in the
basket." As the
wolf leant forward
the frilly bed-
cap slipped and
one of his ears
popped out.

"What big ears you have," said
Little Red Riding Hood.
"All the better to hear you with
my dear," said the wolf, turning
towards her.

"What big eyes you have," said Little Red Riding Hood, beginning to feel just a tiny bit frightened. "All the better to see you with," said the wolf, with a big grin.

"What big teeth you have," said Little Red Riding Hood, now feeling very frightened indeed.

"All the better to EAT you with," said the wolf and he threw back the covers and jumped out of bed.

"You are not my Grandma!" screamed Little Red Riding Hood.

"No, I am not. I am the big bad wolf," growled the wolf in his own voice. "And I am going to eat you up."

"Help! Help!" screamed Little Red Riding Hood as the wolf chased her out of the cottage and into the wood.

The woodcutter heard her screams
and came to the rescue. As soon
as the wolf saw the woodcutter's
big wood-cutting axe, he put his
tail between his legs and ran
away as fast as he could.

Little Red Riding Hood told the woodcutter what had happened. "Where is your Grandma now?" asked the woodcutter.

"I do not know," sobbed Little Red Riding Hood. "Perhaps that horrid wolf has eaten her."

But when they got back to the cottage, they heard the sound of knocking coming from inside the cupboard and a voice asking if it was safe to come out.

"It is me Grandma!" called Little Red Riding Hood.

Only when Grandma was REALLY sure, did she unlock the cupboard door.

"What a lucky escape we have both had," said Little Red Riding Hood as she hugged Grandma.

What a lucky escape indeed.

All these appear in the pages of
the story. Can you find them?

Mother

Little Red Riding Hood

Grandma

flowers

wolf

basket

frilly bed-cap

woodcutter

Use the pictures to tell the story
in your own words, and then draw
your own pictures.

# Three Little Pigs

Once upon a time there were three little pigs. One day, their mother said, "You are old enough to look after yourselves now. It is time for you to go out into the world and build homes of your own."

The three little pigs were very
excited. They walked together as
far as the crossroads and there
they parted.

"Goodbye!" they
called to one another
as they set off in
different directions.

The first little pig always did
things in a hurry. He built himself
a house of straw in the first sunny
field he came to. It was light
and airy and smelt of harvest time
and it swayed gently whenever the

wind blew.
One day he saw a
wicked old wolf
walking across the
field.
"OOOH!" cried the
first little pig
and ran inside his
house of straw.
The wolf knocked
at the door and
called, "Open the
door little pig
and let me in."
He wanted the
little pig for
his dinner.

The first little pig shivered and shook. "By the hair on my chinny chin chin, I will NOT open the door and let you come in."
"Then I will HUFF and I will PUFF and I will blow your house down," growled the wolf.

And he HUFFED and he PUFFED until the house of straw blew away. And THAT was the end of the first little pig.

The second little pig never quite finished anything he started. He built himself a house of sticks in a shady wood. It was full of gaps and creaked whenever the wind blew.

One day he saw a wicked old wolf walking along the woodland path. "OOOH!" cried the second little pig and ran inside his house of sticks. The wolf knocked at the door and called, "Open the door little pig and let me in." He wanted the little pig for his dinner.

The second little pig shivered and shook. "By the hair on my chinny chin chin, I will NOT open the door and let you come in."

"Then I will HUFF and I will PUFF and I will blow your house down," growled the wolf.
And he HUFFED and he PUFFED until the house of sticks tumbled down. And THAT was the end of the second little pig.

The third little
pig always did
everything properly,
even if it took
him a long time.
He built a house
of bricks at the
bottom of a steep
hill. It was snug
and warm and stood
firm and strong.

One day he saw a wicked old wolf walking down the hill.

"OOOH!" cried the third little pig and ran inside his house of bricks.

The wolf knocked at the door and called, "Open the door little pig and let me in." He wanted the little pig for his dinner.

The third little pig shivered and shook. "By the hair on my chinny chin chin, I will NOT open the door and let you come in."
"Then I will HUFF and I will PUFF and I will blow your house down," growled the wolf.

And he HUFFED and he PUFFED and then he HUFFED and PUFFED again.

The wicked old wolf HUFFED and he PUFFED until he was quite out of breath but the house of bricks stood as firm and as strong as a mountain. He could NOT blow it down. If he wanted to catch the little pig he would have to entice him out of the house.

"Little pig," he called. "Meet me in the orchard at ten o'clock tomorrow morning and I will show you where the best apples are."

The third little pig knew how crafty and full of tricks the old wolf was so the next morning he got up very early. He went to the orchard and picked all the best apples and was safely home again by ten o'clock.

When the wicked old wolf got to the orchard and found the best apples gone he knew the third little pig had tricked him. He was very angry but he tried not to show it. He went back to the house of bricks and knocked at the door.

"Are you going to market tomorrow?" he called in his most sly voice.

"Yes I am," said the little pig.

"Then I will meet you at eight o'clock and we can walk there together," said the wolf. "Do not be late."

The third little pig got up very early indeed the next morning. "I will be home from market before the old wolf is even awake," he said. But he was wrong because the wolf got up early too.

The little pig was very frightened when he saw the wolf coming up the hill and he hid inside an empty milk churn which was standing beside the road.

The milk churn began to roll. It rolled down the hill. Faster and faster and faster. It bumped right into the old wolf and sent him sprawling.

"OOOH!" cried the wolf. He could not believe his eyes when he saw the little pig hop from the milk churn and run into the house of bricks and slam the door.

He was very angry
indeed. If he
could not catch
the little pig
outside the house
then he would have
to get into the
house. If the
little pig would
not let him in
through the door
then he would go
down the chimney.

The third little pig heard the wolf
scrambling about on the roof.

"That wicked wolf will NEVER catch me," he cried. He put a pot full of water on the fire and waited. The rumbling and grumbling in the chimney got louder and then suddenly there was a great BIG SPLASH! The wicked old wolf had fallen straight into the pot. And THAT was the end of HIM.

And the third little pig lived happily ever after.

All these appear in the pages
of the story. Can you find them?

three little pigs

wolf

house of straw

house of sticks

house of bricks

apple tree

milk churn

pot of water

Use the pictures to tell the story in your own words, and then draw your own pictures.

# Goldilocks and the Three Bears

Once upon a time there was a father bear, a mother bear, and a baby bear. They lived together in a little cottage in the middle of a wood. Every morning Mother Bear made porridge for breakfast. One morning the porridge was very hot. "Let us go for a walk in the wood while the porridge cools," said Father Bear.

Mother Bear put on her bonnet and out they went into the sunshine.

They pulled the cottage door shut
behind them but it did not latch
properly and presently it swung open.

Goldilocks was out in the wood too that morning. Presently she came to the clearing where the bears' cottage stood. She ran to the open door and peeped inside. "Is there anyone at home?" she called.

She could see that the table was
laid for breakfast. She could see
thin wisps of steam curling from
the three bowls. She wondered what
was in them.
"I will go in and take a quick
peep and then come out again," she
said. "No one will ever know."
She tiptoed across to the table.

Goldilocks was a greedy little girl. When she saw the bowls were full of porridge she picked up a spoon. "I will take just a tiny bit," she said. "No one will ever know." And she took a spoonful of porridge from the largest bowl.

It was very salty.

She did not like it at all.

She took a spoonful of porridge from the middle size bowl.

That was far too sweet.

She did not like that either.

And then she took a spoonful of porridge from the smallest bowl.
It was neither too salty nor too sweet.
It was just right.
And that naughty girl ate it ALL.

There were three wooden chairs with bright patchwork cushions on the seats, beside the fireplace.

Goldilocks decided to try those too.

She sat on the largest chair first.

It was very hard.

She did not like it at all.

She tried the middle size chair.

That was far too soft.

She did not like that either.

And then she tried the smallest chair. It was neither too hard nor too soft. It was just right. But that naughty little girl was NOT right for the chair. She was far too heavy and she wriggled far too much and the little chair broke.

Goldilocks picked herself up from the floor and went up the winding stairs. There were three beds in the bedroom. A large one, a middle size one and a small one.

She tried the large bed first. It was very hard. She did not like it at all. She tried the middle size bed. That was far too soft. She did not like that either. And then she tried the smallest

bed. It was neither too hard nor
too soft. It was just right.
And that naughty little girl curled
up on the bed and went to sleep.

When the three bears came home they knew at once that something was wrong.

"Someone has been tasting my porridge," growled Father Bear with his loud, gruff voice.

"Someone has been tasting my porridge too," said Mother Bear with her soft, gruff voice.

"Someone has been tasting MY porridge," said Baby Bear with his tiny, gruff voice. "And what is more they have eaten it all UP." And poor little Baby Bear burst into tears.

153

Mother Bear mopped Baby Bear's tears dry and Father Bear sat down on his chair to think what was to be done. He jumped up at once. "Someone has been sitting on my chair," he growled with his loud, gruff voice.

"Someone has been sitting on my chair too," growled Mother Bear with her soft, gruff voice.

"Someone has been sitting on MY chair," said Baby Bear in his soft, gruff voice. "And what is more they have broken it." And poor Baby Bear burst into tears all over again.

It made Father Bear and Mother Bear very angry indeed to see Baby Bear cry.

When Mother Bear had mopped Baby
Bear's tears dry all over again
and when Father Bear had promised
to mend the broken chair they all
went upstairs to make sure nothing
else had been broken.

"Someone has been lying on my bed,"
growled Father Bear with his loud,
gruff voice.

"Someone has been lying on my bed too," growled Mother Bear with her soft, gruff voice.

"Someone has been lying on MY bed," said Baby Bear with his tiny, gruff voice. "And what is more . . . she is still there . . . LOOK!"

At that very
moment Goldilocks
woke up and saw
the three bears
looking at her.
She jumped from
the little bed
and ran down the
winding stairs and
out of the cottage
as fast as her
legs would take
her. She did not
stop running until
she got home.

From that day onwards the three bears always made sure the cottage door was firmly closed behind them when they went out. They did not want any more uninvited guests eating their porridge, breaking their chairs or sleeping in their beds.

All these appear in the pages
of the story. Can you find them?

cottage

Father Bear

Mother Bear

Baby Bear

Goldilocks

porridge bowls

chair

bed

Use the pictures to tell the story
in your own words, and then draw
your own pictures.

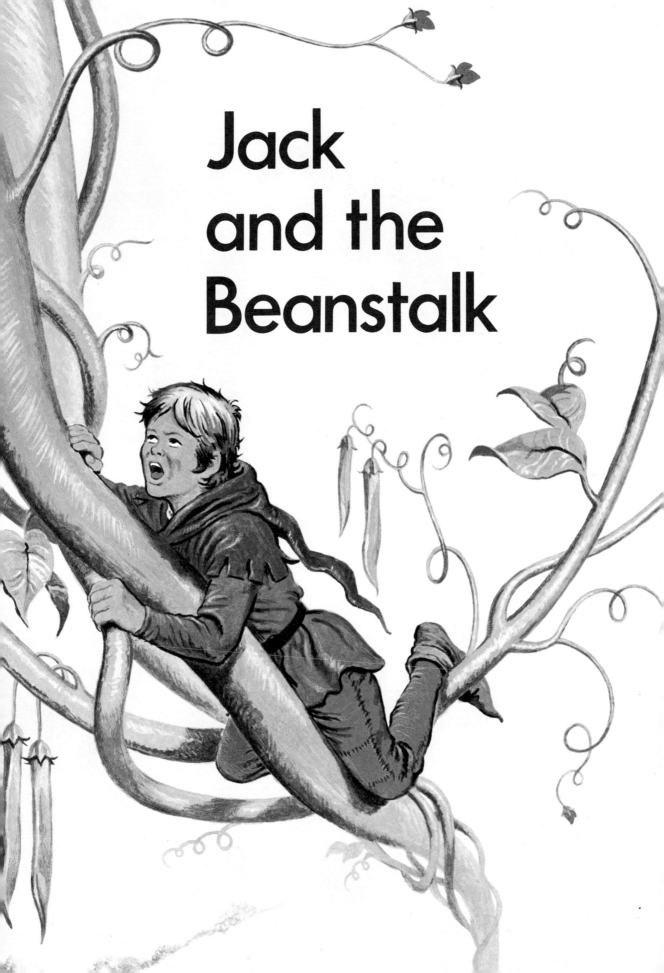

# Jack
# and the
# Beanstalk

Jack and his mother were very poor, and one day, Jack's mother sent him to market to sell their only cow. On the way there he met a man who stopped him and said, "Is your cow for sale?"

"Yes," said Jack.

"Then I will give you five beans for her," said the man.

"That does not seem very much to give for a cow," said Jack.
"But they are not just beans," said the man, "they are magic beans."
"Then I will take them, and you may have the cow," said Jack.

When Jack got home he showed his
mother the beans. She was so
cross she snatched them from his
hand and threw them out of the
window. She would not listen when
Jack said they were magic beans.
"There is no such thing as a
magic bean," she said, and she
sent Jack to bed without any
supper.

How wrong she was.
The beans sprouted
in the night and
grew and grew and
GREW. Next
morning there was
an ENORMOUS
beanstalk growing
outside the window.
"I am going to
see what is at
the top," said
Jack and he began
to climb.
"Do be careful,"
called his mother.

Jack climbed and climbed, higher and still higher, until at last he reached a world above the clouds. He knocked at the first door he came to. It was opened by the wife of a giant. She invited Jack into the house for breakfast.

Jack had just finished eating when
he heard the sound of heavy feet
and a loud voice shouting,
        "FEE FI FO FUM,
        I SMELL THE BLOOD
        OF AN ENGLISHMAN!"
"Quick! Quick!" said the woman.
"That is my husband, the giant.
He eats boys like you for his
breakfast. Quick! Quick! Hide
in the oven."
So, of course,
Jack did. HE
did not want
to be eaten.

The giant was sure he could smell a boy but he could not find him, so he had to make do with oatmeal for his breakfast.

When the giant had scraped his plate clean he called for his hen. Jack was peeping from the oven so he saw what happened next. "Lay hen!" ordered the giant. And straight away the hen laid a beautiful golden egg.

"Mother would like to own a hen like that," thought Jack.

Jack waited until the giant was
asleep, then he crept from his
hiding place. He picked up the
little hen and tucked it inside
his shirt. "You are coming home
with me," he said.

He ran from the house without waking the giant and climbed down the beanstalk. "Look what I have," he called as his mother came to meet him.

Next morning Jack climbed up the beanstalk again, and went back to the giant's house.

"FEE FI FO FUM!"

roared the giant.

"I SMELL THE BLOOD
OF AN ENGLISHMAN!"

This time Jack hid in a drawer and the giant had to make do with oatmeal for his breakfast again. It made him very cross.

When the giant had finished his oatmeal, he called for his harp. "Sing harp!" he ordered. And the harp sang though the giant did not touch its strings once.

"Mother would like a harp that sings by itself," thought Jack.

At last the giant fell asleep, and
Jack crept from his hiding place.
He reached out his hand to pick
up the harp, but as soon as he
touched it the harp called loudly,
"Master! Master! Wake up!"
Jack quickly pushed the harp into
his shirt to muffle its voice,
but he was too late.
The giant jumped
from his chair
with a loud roar.

"FEE FI FO FUM!" he cried, "I KNEW I COULD SMELL THE BLOOD OF AN ENGLISHMAN!"

Jack dodged between the giant's
fingers and ran as fast as he
could to the top of the beanstalk.
"FEE FI FO FUM!" shouted the
giant. He was in a terrible rage.
"FEE FI FO FUM!"

As Jack climbed down the beanstalk he could feel it shaking and trembling. He could feel the giant's breath blowing like a hot fierce wind down his neck. "FEE FI FO FUM!"

Jack's mother heard all the noise and came running. She was very frightened when she saw the giant. "Quick! Quick! Give me the axe!" shouted Jack as he jumped the last few feet to the ground. There was no time to lose. He took the axe from his mother, and with one mighty blow he cut right through the beanstalk.

It fell to the ground with a great crash, and made a hole so deep that neither the beanstalk nor the giant were ever seen again.

As for Jack and his mother, they lived happily ever after, and with a hen that laid golden eggs and a harp that sang by itself they were never poor again.

All these appear in the pages of the story. Can you find them?

cow

oven

Jack

beanstalk

giant

hen

harp

axe

Use the pictures to tell the story
in your own words, and then draw
your own pictures.

# Puss in Boots

Once there was a miller who had three sons. When he died he left his eldest son the mill. He left his second eldest son the donkey. He had nothing to leave John, his youngest son, except the cat.

John's brothers laughed. "You will never make a fortune with a cat," they said.

"Master" said the cat when John and
he were alone. "Buy me a pair of
boots and I WILL make you a
fortune." It was plain to see the
cat was no ordinary cat.

John did as the
cat asked. He
bought him a pair
of boots. The
cat put them on.

"Now give me a
sack and I will
go hunting," said
Puss in Boots,
as he was to be
known from then
on.

Puss in Boots went
into the forest.
He caught a rabbit.
Instead of taking
it home to John
he took it to the
King's palace.
"I have a present
for the King," he
said.

"I am Puss in Boots," he said to the King. "I have brought you a present from my master, the Marquis of Carrabas."

"Thank you very much," said the King. Kings are like everyone else. They like getting presents.

Puss in Boots went hunting every
day. Everything he caught he took
to the King. Every day he said,
"This is a present from my master
the Marquis of Carrabas."
One day, the King said, "I would
like to meet your master. I will
call my coach. You can take me
to see him."

"I cannot ride with you," said Puss in Boots. "I have some business to attend to. I will meet you at my master's castle."
"Very well!" said the King.

The Princess said she would ride with the King. They got into the coach and set off.

On the way they passed some men working in the fields. "Who owns this land?" called the King.
"The Marquis of Carrabas!" answered the men. Puss in Boots had already passed that way. HE had told the men what to say if the King spoke to them.

There were men cutting wood in the forest. "Who owns THIS land?" called the King.

"The Marquis of Carrabas!" replied the wood cutters. Puss in Boots had told THEM what to say too.

"The Marquis of Carrabas must be a very rich man," said the King.

When Puss in Boots got home he called to John. "Quick master! Go to the river and bathe."

"Why?" asked John.

"Just do as I say!" said Puss in Boots.

John was puzzled but he did as he was told. He was even more puzzled when Puss ran off with his clothes and hid them under a bush.

"Help! Help!" called Puss in Boots
when he saw the King's coach
coming. "Help! Help! My master,
the Marquis of Carrabas, is
drowning!"

"Someone has stolen my master's clothes," said Puss, when John was rescued.

The King lent John his cloak and invited him to ride in the royal coach.

"The Marquis of Carrabas is very handsome," thought the Princess.

"My master's castle is just over the next hill," said Puss in Boots. "I will run on ahead and prepare for your arrival."

The castle over
the next hill
really belonged to
a wicked ogre.
Puss in Boots
knocked at the
door. The ogre
opened it himself.
"I have heard you
are very clever,"
said Puss in Boots.
"I have come to
see if it's true."
"I AM very clever!"
roared the ogre.

"I can change myself into ANYTHING
I please." The ogre snapped his
fingers and changed himself into a
lion. He growled at Puss in Boots.
Puss pretended not to be afraid.

"It's EASY to change into something big," said Puss in Boots. "I don't suppose you can change yourself into something as small as . . . as small as a mouse!"

"OH, YES I CAN!" roared the ogre. AND HE DID. But before he could change back again Puss in Boots gobbled him up. And that was the end of the ogre.

"You have a new master now," said Puss in Boots to the people who lived in the castle. "He is the Marquis of Carrabas. The King is bringing him here now. We must prepare a feast."

"Hooray for the King!" they shouted. "Hooray for the Marquis!"

"HOORAY FOR PUSS IN BOOTS!"

When the King's coach arrived
Puss in Boots was waiting at the
castle door.
"Welcome! Welcome to the castle of
the Marquis of Carrabas," he said.
"Who IS this Marquis of Carrabas?"

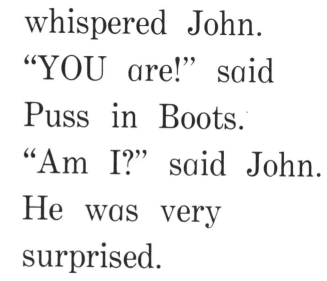

whispered John.
"YOU are!" said
Puss in Boots.
"Am I?" said John.
He was very
surprised.

John married the Princess, and they lived in the castle. Many years later, they moved into the palace and John became King. Puss in Boots HAD made John's fortune for him, just as he said he would.

All these appear in the pages of
the story. Can you find them?

cat

boots

sack

rabbit

Use the pictures to tell the story
in your own words, and then draw
your own pictures.

King

ogre

castle

mouse